AF228482

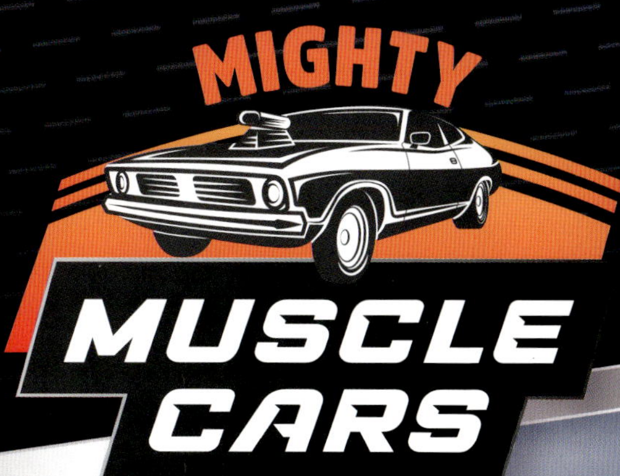

MIGHTY MUSCLE CARS

PONTIAC TRANS AM

Scott Wilken

Big Buddy Books

An Imprint of Abdo Publishing
abdobooks.com

abdobooks.com

Published by Abdo Publishing, a division of ABDO, PO Box 398166, Minneapolis, Minnesota 55439. Copyright © 2021 by Abdo Consulting Group, Inc. International copyrights reserved in all countries. No part of this book may be reproduced in any form without written permission from the publisher. Big Buddy Books™ is a trademark and logo of Abdo Publishing.

Printed in China
082020
012021

Design: Christa Schneider, Mighty Media, Inc.
Production: Mighty Media, Inc.
Editor: Megan Borgert-Spaniol

Cover Photograph: WMrapids/Wikimedia Commons

Interior Photographs: americancar/Wikimedia Commons, p. 28 (1969); Chad Horwedel/Flickr, pp. 12, 13, 14, 15, 20, 21, 28 (1973), 29 (2002); Glen Bowman/Flickr, pp. 18, 19, 29 (1993); mashleymorgan/Flickr, pp. 10, 11; Michel Curi/Flickr, pp. 16, 17; Royalbroil/Wikimedia Commons, pp. 22, 23; Shutterstock Images, pp. 8, 9, 21, 24, 25, 26, 27, 28, 29; Sicnag/Flickr, pp. 4, 5; WMrapids/Wikimedia Commons, p. 7

Design Elements: Shutterstock Images

Library of Congress Control Number: 2020931634

Publisher's Cataloging-in-Publication Data
Names: Wilken, Scott, author.
Title: Pontiac Trans Am / by Scott Wilken
Description: Minneapolis, Minnesota : Abdo Publishing, 2021 | Series: Mighty muscle cars | Includes online resources and index
Identifiers: ISBN 9781532193286 (lib. bdg.) | ISBN 9781098211929 (ebook)
Subjects: LCSH: Muscle cars--Juvenile literature. | Motor vehicles--Juvenile literature. | Automobiles--Customizing--Juvenile literature. | Hot rods--Juvenile literature.
Classification: DDC 629.222--dc23

CONTENTS

TRANS AM VICTORY

Heat rises from the drag strip in Las Vegas, Nevada. A 1989 Pontiac Trans Am and a 1987 Ford Mustang take their places at the starting line. Tires squeal. Both cars are off!

For the next one-quarter mile (0.4 km), the cars are neck and neck. Then the Trans Am takes the lead. Its driver clocks in at 14.9 seconds. The Trans Am has won!

DID YOU KNOW?

In a drag race, two cars race on a straight track called a drag strip. Most drag strips are one-eighth mile (0.2 km) or one-quarter mile (0.4 km) long.

GTA · 383
VIC

AMERICAN MUSCLE

The Pontiac Trans Am was one of the most iconic muscle cars ever built. Muscle cars are American high-performance cars. They are built for power and speed.

The first muscle car came out in 1949. Muscle cars soon became widely popular in the 1960s. They were made for drag racing. But most could also be driven on city streets.

DID YOU KNOW?

Horsepower (hp) is a measure of how powerful an engine is. One hp equals the power needed to lift a 550-pound (249 kg) weight up one foot (0.3 m) in one second.

PONTIAC TRANS AM
FAST FACTS

Manufacturer: General Motors (GM)

Model years: 1969–2002

Top speed: 165 miles per hour (265 km/h)

Top horsepower: 335 hp

Top acceleration: 0 to 60 miles per hour
(96 km/h) in 5.0 seconds

PONTIAC PAST

Car company General Motors (GM) started the Pontiac brand in 1926. Pontiac cars were made in Pontiac, Michigan. They were affordable everyday cars.

Pontiac started making muscle cars in the 1960s. The first was the 1964 Pontiac GTO. Then came the 1967 Pontiac Firebird. These cars launched Pontiac's muscle car **legacy**.

DID YOU KNOW?

The city and the car brand were named *Pontiac* after a famous Native American chief.

1967 Pontiac Firebird

FIREBIRD TRANSFORMATION

The Pontiac Trans Am **debuted** at the Chicago Auto Show in 1969. The Trans Am was a new type of Firebird. It had a stronger **suspension** and more powerful engine. Fewer than 700 Trans Ams were made in 1969. But the new model would later become one of the most popular muscle cars.

DID YOU KNOW?

The Trans Am was named after the Trans Am Series. This race series is run by the Sports Car Club of America.

The first Trans Ams were white with blue racing stripes.

SUPER DUTY

The second-**generation** Trans Am came out in 1970. In the first few years, sales were so low that GM nearly stopped making it. But two changes in 1973 saved the Trans Am. The first was an even more powerful engine. The 455 Super Duty engine could handle more than regular street driving. It was built for track performance!

A 1973 Trans Am with a 455 Super Duty engine

SCREAMING CHICKEN

The second big change to the Trans Am in 1973 was a new **decal**. It was of a large bird. The image covered the entire hood of the car. People soon started calling the decal the "screaming chicken." This new look made the Trans Am even more popular.

DID YOU KNOW?

Pontiac made a 1976 Special **Edition** Trans Am. Some of the models were T-tops. A T-top has two removable roof sections, leaving a center strip of the roof in place.

The 1976 Special Edition Trans Am was black with a golden screaming chicken.

THIRD GENERATION

The third-**generation** Trans Am came out in 1982. Starting that year, Pontiac no longer made its own engines. The Trans Am was now built with the engines from another GM car brand, Chevrolet. However, the Trans Am remained popular. It had a cool, sleek look and was fun to drive.

The Trans Am was the pace car for the 1989 Indianapolis 500 car race. In a race, the pace car leads the competing cars to control their speed.

FINAL GENERATION

Fourth-**generation** Trans Ams were built from 1993 to 2002. During these years, the Trans Am was known for its powerful engines. These included the LT1 engine in 1993 and the LS1 engine in 1998. These engines made Trans Ams some of the most exciting cars to drive.

A 1994 Trans Am is one of more than 400 classic cars at the Haynes International Motor Museum in England.

UNDER THE HOOD

PONTIAC FIREBIRD TRANS AM

The last Pontiac Firebird Trans Am came out in 2002. Like many previous models, it had a V8 engine. That means the engine had eight **cylinders**. The more cylinders an engine has, the more powerful it is.

CAR ENGINES 101

Car engines turn the energy in gasoline into motion. Fuel and air are pumped into the engine's **cylinders**. A spark creates an explosion. The explosion pushes the **piston** down to turn the **crankshaft**. This is a bit like a foot pushing down on a bicycle pedal. At high speed, these explosions happen thousands of times a minute!

ON THE TRACK

Muscle car fans have loved watching the Trans Am roar down the racetrack. In 1982, the car appeared in the Trans Am racing series it was named after. Driver Elliott Forbes-Robinson drove the car to a championship win.

From 1996 to 2006, the Trans Am was the chosen car for the International Race of Champions. In this race, every driver rode the same type of car. This allowed drivers to compare their racing skills.

Matt Kenseth won the 2004 International Race of Champions in a Firebird Trans Am.

STAR CAR

The Trans Am was a hit on the big screen during the 1970s and 1980s. Actor Burt Reynolds loved the car. In several hit movies, Reynolds played characters who drove Trans Ams. These movies helped draw attention to the Trans Am.

From 1982 to 1986, a Trans Am starred in the TV show *Knight Rider*. It played a **high-tech** car called KITT. KITT could drive itself and even talk to people!

KITT from *Knight Rider*

MAKING A COMEBACK

GM ended the Pontiac brand in 2009. However, in 2011, Trans Am Worldwide bought the rights to the Trans Am. This company turns Chevrolet Camaro cars into Trans Ams. The company's leaders want the Trans Am's muscle car **legacy** to keep going strong!

Trans Am Worldwide displayed a new Trans Am Super Duty at the Los Angeles Auto Show in 2019.

TIMELINE

General Motors (GM) created the Pontiac brand.

1926

The Pontiac Firebird Trans Am **debuted** at the Chicago Auto Show.

1969

The 455 Super Duty engine and "screaming chicken" hood **decal** made the Trans Am more popular.

1973

1967

Pontiac built the first Firebird.

1970

Pontiac debuted the second **generation** of Trans Ams.

Pontiac **debuted** the third-**generation** Trans Am.

The last Pontiac Firebird Trans Am rolled out of the factory.

1982

2002

1993

2009

2011

Pontiac debuted the fourth-generation Trans Am.

GM ended the Pontiac brand.

Trans Am Worldwide bought the rights to the Trans Am name. The company started turning Chevrolet Camaros into Trans Ams.

crankshaft—a long, metal rod that transfers energy from the engine through the transmission and eventually to the wheels.

cylinder—a shaft in which a piston of an engine moves.

debut—to appear for the first time or present something for the first time.

decal—a label or sticker with a picture or design on it.

edition—a version of a product.

generation—a class of objects created from an earlier type.

high-tech—having highly advanced capabilities given by the practical application of knowledge.

legacy—something important or meaningful handed down from previous generations or from the past.

piston—a part in an engine that moves up and down inside
the cylinder.

suspension—a system of devices that supports the upper part of
an automobile on its axles.

ONLINE RESOURCES

To learn more about the Pontiac Trans Am, please
visit **abdobooklinks.com** or scan this QR code.
These links are routinely monitored and updated
to provide the most current information available.

INDEX